HEROES OF RACING

DALE EARNHARDT, SR.

The Intimidator

by James MacDonald

Enslow Publishers, Inc.

40 Industrial Road
Box 398
Berkeley Heights, NJ 07922
USA
http://www.enslow.com

Copyright © 2009 by Enslow Publishers, Inc.

Library of Congress Cataloging-in-Publication Data
MacDonald, James, 1971 Oct. 8-
    Dale Earnhardt, Sr. : the intimidator / James MacDonald.
       p. cm. — (Heroes of racing)
    Summary: "A biography of American NASCAR driver Dale Earnhardt, Sr"—Provided by publisher.
    Includes bibliographical references and index.
    ISBN-13: 978-0-7660-3297-2
    ISBN-10: 0-7660-3297-3
    1. Earnhardt, Dale, 1951-2001—Juvenile literature. 2. Automobile racing drivers—United States—Biography—Juvenile literature. I. Title.
    GV1032.E18M33 2009
    796.72092—dc22
    [B]
                                              2008007692

Printed in the United States of America

10 9 8 7 6 5 4 3 2 1

To Our Readers: We have done our best to make sure all Internet addresses in this book were active and appropriate when we went to press. However, the author and the publisher have no control over and assume no liability for the material available on those Internet sites or on other Web sites they may link to. Any comments or suggestions can be sent by e-mail to comments@enslow.com or to the address on the back cover.

Disclaimer: This publication is not affiliated with, endorsed by, or sponsored by NASCAR. NASCAR®, WINSTON CUP®, NEXTEL CUP, BUSCH SERIES and CRAFTSMAN TRUCK SERIES are trademarks owned or controlled by the National Association for Stock Car Auto Racing, Inc., and are registered where indicated.

♻ Enslow Publishers, Inc. is committed to printing our books on recycled paper. The paper in every book contains between 10% to 30% post-consumer waste (PCW). The cover board on the outside of each book contains 100% PCW. Our goal is to do our part to help young people and the environment too!

Photo credits: Chris O'Meara/AP Images, 5, 11, 27; David Mills/The Lakeland Ledger/AP Images, 8; Gary O'Brien/The Charlotte Observer/AP Images, 16; Spencer Jones/AP Images, 19; Rusty Burroughs/AP Images, 22; Amy Conn/AP Images, 31; Chuck Burton/AP Images, 36; Bill Scott/AP Images, 41; Terry Renna/AP Images, 47, 54; Grant Halverson/AP Images, 51; Adam Nadel/AP Images, 59; Rusty Kennedy/AP Images, 61; RacingOne/Getty Images, 64; Mark Foley/AP Images, 69; Justin Sutcliffe/AP Images, 75; Peter Cosgrove/AP Images, 81; Tom Strattman/AP Images, 84; Dale Atkins/AP Images, 92; Greg Suvino/AP Images, 102; John Raoux/AP Images, 107.

Cover Photo: Chris O'Meara/AP Images

CONTENTS

Of all the finishes in the history of driving fast cars for sport, few could have matched the one that took place on February 15, 1998.

The setting was the Daytona 500. It is the first race of the NASCAR season and is always the biggest event on its calendar. In some ways, race teams spend their three-month off-season preparing for annual showdown known as "The Great American Race."

In his own way, veteran driver Dale Earnhardt had spent nineteen years preparing for it.

Dale Earnhardt sits in the window of his race car at Daytona International Speedway.

He had long since overcome humble beginnings to become the most recognizable name in NASCAR. The son of a "short-track" racer, Earnhardt had won millions of dollars and was followed by millions of fans. From the second he climbed into a stock car in 1975, he was a race car driver.

Legions cheered for him. They relished the sight of his black No. 3 working through traffic and gaining the lead. Earnhardt had a way of making his own room on the track. He drove his car as if it had wide shoulders and sharp elbows. If there were a few drivers in his way, he knew he just might have to move them aside.

DID YOU KNOW?

No one had won more preliminary races at Daytona than Earnhardt.

The aggressive driving style earned him nicknames such as "the Intimidator" and "the Man in Black." Fans ate it up. They liked to think he raced as hard as humanly possible toward the next turn, the next finish line, and the next championship. They appreciated his rough-around-the-edges image.

There were vicious wrecks. There were hard times. And, there were storybook finishes and story-book flameouts. Not much for outward emotion, Earnhardt just showed up the following weekend ready to race again. No whining. No tears.

YEARNING TO WIN

Some of the "Intimidator" and "Man in Black" publicity may have been produced by a touch of acting, but Earnhardt was pure race car driver, through and through.

By 1998, he had won just about everything a NASCAR driver could. He had won the points championship seven times. In the previous ten seasons, he earned more than $13 million racing. He was rich beyond his wildest dreams and considered as cool as they come. Even without the swagger, he would have been a legend on results alone. He had won almost every race on the NASCAR circuit. Earnhardt was known for succeeding in most races at Daytona International Speedway. But there was one race there each year that he simply could not win. That it was the biggest, most important race of the year left a big hole in his list of career accomplishments.

It was a hole that threatened to swallow a brilliant career. Earnhardt had been one of the most accomplished racers at Daytona's famed track. He had won nine consecutive qualifying races in preparation for the Daytona 500. He had won more races, in all kinds of different cars, at Daytona's various events than anyone.

He was the biggest name in the sport. But he had never won the big one, the Daytona 500. In nineteen previous starts, the NASCAR legend had never won the sport's biggest race.

QUOTABLE
"I don't sit there and analyze things. I go out and make 'em happen."

— Dale Earnhardt

Earnhardt encountered yet another roadblock when his car flipped onto its roof during a crash at the 1997 Daytona 500.

He challenged often, but his failures were epic. He blew an engine late in the 1986 race. He blew a tire very late in the 1990 race. He hit a bird in the 1991 race. He was passed on the final lap in 1993. He finished second during a last-lap duel again in 1996.

FAN FAVORITE

By 1998, he was not only a favorite of his own fans, but a favorite for so many fans who had begun rooting for a new generation of drivers. There were now Jeff Gordon fans, Bobby Labonte fans, and Jeff Burton fans.

At that point, Earnhardt was forty-six years old. He would have disagreed, but time was no longer on his side. NASCAR is kind to its legends, but it was becoming a younger man's game every year. The defending Daytona 500 champion, Gordon, was only twenty-six at the time. Earnhardt had taken to calling Gordon "Wonder Boy" against Gordon's wishes. Earnhardt clearly still had his edge. Yet the opportunities to win the Daytona 500 were dwindling. On the morning of February 15, 1998, Earnhardt hadn't won a NASCAR race in his previous fifty-nine starts.

He was more than ready to play hero in the fortieth running of the Daytona 500. "To go out and win the Daytona 500 in our 20th year and NASCAR's 50th would be a heck of an honor and an accomplishment," he told *The New York Times*. "It's tough to go out every year and not win. If you were a basketball or football team, everybody would be getting fired."[1]

Television coverage of the event kicked off NASCAR's fiftieth season. In the opening remarks, a voice-over considered Earnhardt among the favorites: "Will it be the man who has had his eye on the checkered flag through 20 years of frustration . . . Dale Earnhardt?"[2]

By the seventeenth lap, Earnhardt had found his way to the front. Gordon was also very strong. In Gordon's own No. 24, NASCAR's young gun led fifty-six of the race's scheduled 200 laps. But he had fallen off the pace with a few laps remaining. Earnhardt, on the other hand, had been ticking off the laps as the race leader.

TRACK FACT

Bobby Labonte, who finished second at the 1998 Daytona 500, had won the pole entering the event.

LEADING THE 500

He'd been there before, of course, leading late in the Daytona 500, so winning wasn't exactly in the bag. Nearing the 199th lap, the No. 3 car blew by a lapped car and the rest of the field tried to do the same.

The fans had been on their feet for at least a few laps, cheering and hollering. The voices of nearly 185,000 screaming fans from the grandstands drowned out the roar of the engines as Earnhardt drove the best he knew how. The No. 3 kept on. Earnhardt was managing to keep all that traffic, all the years of disappointment, and all that bad luck behind him. The best story in racing was tearing up the pavement on the way to making Earnhardt's own sweet history.

Dale Earnhardt was all smiles after winning the Daytona 500 in 1998. It was his lone title in the storied race.

Suddenly, there was trouble in Turn 2. The yellow caution flag was waved. When a caution is called, racers are not allowed to pass each other. With only one lap left in the race, that meant that whoever was leading at the end of the 199th lap would be the winner. Earnhardt had to grind out those next few turns with Bobby Labonte and Jeremy Mayfield trying like crazy to ruin the happiest ending.

The crowd roared louder. Labonte and Mayfield were running out of pavement. Earnhardt was going to pull it off, at long last.

The toughest guy with the toughest story admitted his eyes watered up toward the end. It had nothing to do with the record prize money, either. The $1,059,105 was the most money ever awarded for a NASCAR win, but wasn't worth nearly as much as the moment. It was a lifetime achievement award.

Earnhardt cruised down pit road on his way to Victory Lane. Every member of every NASCAR team came out to pay their respects. It was an unprecedented scene.

TRACK FACT

Earnhardt led the final sixty laps of the 1998 Daytona 500.

"I'm excited for Earnhardt," Gordon said afterward. "We all want to win the Daytona 500. But as many times as he's been so close, so close, he deserves it and he's earned it."[3]

At that very point, Earnhardt eased his car toward the infield and gunned the engine. The No. 3 tore a donut into the grass. After a second donut, Earnhardt made his long-awaited way to Victory Lane.

He crawled out from his car. The Man in Black was wearing his white racing suit. He climbed to the roof and raised his arms. In an emotional television interview, Earnhardt let his feelings out. "The Daytona 500 is ours. We won it. We won it. We won it!" he exclaimed.[4]

Later, Earnhardt opened up further.

"Now, I won't have to answer that question anymore," he told *Sports Illustrated*. "The years of disappointment, the close calls, all the chapters have been written. Now, the 20th chapter is in. To win this race is something you can't, I mean, you really can't put into words. . . . It's everything you've ever worked hard to do, and you've finally accomplished it."[5]

Ralph Dale Earnhardt was born on April 29, 1951, in Kannapolis, North Carolina. His father was Ralph Lee Earnhardt, and his mother's maiden name was Martha Coleman. Kannapolis wasn't famous for much then, but it was well known in the area for its textile mills.

It wouldn't be long before the city would become forever linked to the Earnhardt name.

As lore and luck might have it, Martha and Ralph raised Dale on Sedan Avenue in Kannapolis. Around the corner, Sedan intersected with Coach Street on the south and with V-8 Street to the north.

There were many automotive references in Kannapolis. A few blocks from Dale's childhood home sits a grid of streets named Cadillac, Chrysler, Dodge, Packard, Ford, Plymouth, Buick, and Chevrolet.

Some stories are good from the very beginning. Earnhardt's life is one such story. He became one of the most compelling tales in modern sports history. The fact that he was born in a place with its own "Car Town" just seems appropriate.

A modest white house on Sedan is the Earnhardt version of a fairy tale beginning. It is the first chapter in a hardscrabble and hard-earned American Dream. The American Dream . . . Earnhardt style.

Earnhardt's success was not just about where he lived.

THE KID FROM KANNAPOLIS

Many kids had grown up on those streets in Kannapolis in the 1950s. Their childhoods were mostly routine with friends and sports and bikes. Some kids may even have tuned in to the buzz about fast rides and fast engines among a car-crazy set of locals and mechanics.

There was only one Dale Earnhardt. There was only one kid whose career sped from Kannapolis and wound up in headlines and on magazine covers and on a

Earnhardt's hometown of Kannapolis, North Carolina, was known for its textile mills.

Wheaties box because of the way he drove a car. Only Dale Earnhardt did everything in his power to put his name in lights.

The journey started with his father. Ralph Lee Earnhardt was also born in Kannapolis. He dropped out of school in the sixth grade, which he had always hoped Dale wouldn't do, and was married to Martha in the late 1940s. By the time Dale was born, his father was only twenty-three, and the couple already had three children.

For new dads in Kannapolis—almost all dads, really—the career path back then was straightforward.

With the textile industry in their backyard, that's where many locals worked.

Ralph was getting by at a mill when he met Martha. He may have gained experience with a typical local job, but he was ready for another kind of career track, one with a little more horsepower.

While he had a job, Ralph's life was about cars. Over the years, he had been turning wrenches and helping a local shop cook up some of the fastest cars in the area. The mechanics there could turn a plain old car into a rocket on wheels.

Racing was barely a hobby for most. Ralph set out to make it his living. At the time, such a decision was nearly unheard of. This was long before the days when first-place money could support the average household for a year. Driving for purses at small raceways and dirt tracks during the 1950s wasn't the way to worldwide fame.

"Earnhardt was a rare man in many ways," Ken Willis wrote for the *Daytona Beach News-Journal* in 2002, "but mostly because he chucked the lunch box and time sheet and went racing full time. Unheard of back then. . . . A Carolina short-tracker just doesn't quit work and drive for a living. Not if he wants to eat regularly."[1]

Martha wasn't sure what to think, but she agreed with the plan. Ralph made up his mind.

With his wife supportive enough to let him chase cars for a living, he became one of the area's top drivers.

In 1956, he won the NASCAR Sportsman Division championship.

"That circuit, mostly in the Carolinas and Georgia, was poor and gritty, and Daddy Ralph was toughest of the tough, a 'driver's driver' who won by never giving an inch," according to a 1987 article in *Sports Illustrated*.[2]

MIDDLE KID
Dale grew up as the middle of Ralph and Martha's five children.

Ralph worked on his own cars in a shop he had fashioned behind the house on Sedan Avenue. And he worked hard. He wasn't much for small talk. He was more of a "lone rider" who tried to keep his shop and his car clean.[3] As NASCAR icon H. A. Humpy Wheeler said, "He was driving the family bank. . . . He couldn't afford to wreck."[4]

Ralph made the most of every part he could find. The atmosphere set quite an example for his son. He left lasting impressions about work ethic, values, and what was important in life. Among them, Dale remembered his father saying: "When you leave here, all you're gonna have is your name and your word.

Dale's father Ralph (in car No. 75) spins out in a 1962 race in Darlington, South Carolina.

If that's not any good, then you're not much good. . . . I want to be remembered as much for that as for being a great racer—being a good father, for one, but also a fair person in life, fair to other people."[5]

Watching Ralph at the track taught its share of lessons. While Dale was tearing around on his tricycle, his father was racing three, four, and five times a week.

HIS FATHER'S SON

"Dale Sr. remembers the excitement of it all," wrote Leigh Montville, the *Sports*

MAKING A LIVING
Racing was barely a hobby for most. Ralph set out to make it his living.

Illustrated writer who worked on a 1999 piece for the magazine and later a Dale Earnhardt biography. "The races were mostly in North Carolina and Georgia, mostly on Saturday nights. Ralph would win, and the family would drive home and there would be a party. Ham steaks would be fried next to eggs, a country breakfast at midnight, and his aunt and uncle, neighbors and friends would gather to talk about the race until dawn."[6]

For a kid who idolized his dad, those memories are hard to beat. When Ralph racked up his obscure titles, Dale was part roadie, part groupie, and fully involved. Before his teens, Dale was already traveling to races and lending a hand. He was helping fix his dad's cars. He couldn't get enough of it.

In that respect, he was similar to his father. More than one time, in the middle of the night, Ralph woke up and headed out to work on his car in the shop. "I just thought of something I want to change," Dale recalled his father telling his mother.[7]

Throughout his childhood, as Dale grew, so did his appetite for cars and racing. Racing agreed with the young Earnhardt.

"He was always all over Ralph's car," said Jim Hunter, a racetrack president who knew the father-and-son duo when he was a reporter in those days. "If Ralph changed a gear, he'd be helping him. He was his daddy's helper. When it came to race cars, Dale was one of those who knew them from top to bottom, side to side, and back to front. He had probably forgotten more about race cars than most of today's drivers will ever know."[8]

In Dale's heart, racing was the best living ever.

"I wanted to race—that's all I ever wanted to do," Dale said. "I didn't care about work or school or anything. All I wanted to do was to work on race cars and then drive race cars."[9]

School wasn't his thing. He was smart, but just not in a traditional setting. Classrooms were his distraction. He was a living-learner, and a man of action.

> **QUOTABLE**
> "[Ralph] was driving the family bank. . . . He couldn't afford to wreck."
>
> — **Humpy Wheeler**

REAL SHOP CLASS

The shop and the racetrack were Dale's favorite places to learn. He had the luxury—and the curse—of knowing exactly what he wanted to do at a young age. "I didn't like school. I wanted to be home working on dad's race cars," Dale said later. "I didn't like school. I wanted to be home cleaning up the shop. I didn't like school. I would just as soon be washing wrenches."[10]

Humpy Wheeler (right), conversing with Dale Earnhardt Jr. and Jimmie Johnson, saw Dale Sr. get his start in racing.

Eventually, Dale made the decision to quit school. He dropped out before finishing the ninth grade. Dale's father was very disappointed, but stubborn Dale lived up to his nickname, "Ironhead," and didn't return.

Stubbornness turned out to serve Dale well later in life on the racetrack. His determination, ambition, talent, confidence, and the nerves to indulge his will to win would also be important.

But the decision to drop out was one that he would later regret. At the time, however, it seemed like the right thing to do. As it turned out, it was the first in a string of decisions made by Dale that would complicate his life. In spite of all of his qualities as a race car driver, he seemed to want to put roadblocks in his own way.

Soon after dropping out, Dale would throw another few obstacles in his path. Especially in his early years, Dale had a knack for driving up the odds that he would even make a living, let alone a legend, out of racing.

DID YOU KNOW?

Ralph also recorded many strong finishes in occasional starts on NASCAR's top circuit. In fact, he finished seventeenth overall in 1961.

MERELY A DREAM

The next stage of Dale's life would be his most trying.

It started with disappointing his father by dropping out of school at sixteen. His sights set on racing, Dale left the formal education system behind.

Later in life, he'd tell everyone who would listen to stay in school. Dropping out became one of his biggest regrets. He wished he hadn't disappointed his dad. And he learned how important an education is to everyone. At age sixteen, however, it is not always easy to see that far into the future. For a boy who had a rugged race car driver for a dad and the roar of an engine in his heart, it was nearly impossible.

With his visions of cars and wrenches and racing, Dale didn't have the time or inclination for much else. Unfortunately, life at 100 m.p.h. has a way of running off course. Soon, Dale added a few more dangerous decisions.

A MARRIED MAN

In 1968, he married. He was only seventeen at the time of his wedding to Latane Brown. In 1969, they had a son, Kerry Dale Earnhardt.

By 1970, that marriage had ended. The pair went their separate ways, and Kerry would later be adopted by Latane's second husband. Dale could hardly afford to help.

Earnhardt wasn't learning from life's lessons, either. Instead, he created more complications.

In 1971, Earnhardt married again. He and Brenda Gee, who was also from a racing family, had two children. Their daughter Kelley was born in 1972 and son Dale Jr. was born in 1974. By the time Dale Sr.'s racing dreams were closer to reality in the late 1970s, he and Brenda had divorced.

Ralph began his own family life balancing it against racing. Dale's choices proved he wanted to race even more. It seemed as if Ralph wanted to race as much as his life allowed. It seemed as if Dale wanted to race no matter what.

Wives and ex-wives and children are heavy responsibilities at any age. And here was Dale, barely into his twenties in Kannapolis, catching them up in the teeth of the storm that was driving him to race cars.

There was barely a payoff to racing in those knock-down, drag-out days. Ralph barely made it work, and he was a seasoned veteran.

BAD IDEA
Dale realized as an adult that dropping out of school was a foolish decision.

In addition to the Intimidator, another nickname choice for Dale could have been the Determinator. Without his high-revving engine, Dale's early decisions could have brought down a handful of lives.

Dale Earnhardt wouldn't have it that way. Racing wound up financially saving those around him. Unfortunately, it took nearly ten years of short tracks, dusty lanes, and empty pockets.

One of Dale's most famous quotes, and there are hundreds, is: "I started racing full time, and that's when I started starving to death."[1]

Dale Earnhardt's road to the top of the NASCAR circuit included a lot of learning along the way.

He even made the move to racing hard on himself. Had he stayed in school, his father may have been more encouraging. As it was, his relationship cooled with his father.

Dale's career started to form during the early 1970s. His grip on the wheel tightened as he neared twenty-two. His grip loosened on everything else, however. His paying jobs were dead-enders—he tried mill work, garage work, welding work, and other short-timer work. He accumulated debt.

He often raced on loans he would try to pay back with winnings. If that sounds odd, there was a method behind what might have seemed like madness. Dale was calculating, not crazy. Essentially, he was betting on himself.

DID YOU KNOW?

Dale's first car was almost Pink Panther pink after a paint-mixing accident.

Dale is quoted in a 1995 newspaper article as saying his family "probably should have been on welfare," and that they "didn't have money to buy groceries."[2]

The circumstances would get even worse.

In the midst of all those dramas, Earnhardt suffered the greatest loss in his life. The news came suddenly and there was no way to prepare for its impact.

On September 26, 1973, Ralph Earnhardt passed away. Dale was only twenty-two.

Making matters worse, the two had patched up their bond as Dale showed promise on the track. Their relationship had matured from when "Ralph's Boy" would root for his dad from the top of the family's truck.

LEARNING FROM DAD

They were often at the same tracks together, racing in different divisions. Something closer to an adult connection formed. Ralph still taught, however, and Dale still listened. "Dad knew that driving skill came naturally," Earnhardt said. "So he would make me aware of my mistakes and try to guide me in the right direction. . . .

"He had his influence. He gave me the positive attitude. He guided me and set the stage for the kind of driver I am."[3]

Ralph may not have known what might become of his son, but he surely saw his kid was good. It was hard for casual fans to miss the hard-charging youngster. He seemed wise beyond his years on the track.

DETERMINED

In addition to the Intimidator, another nickname choice for Dale could have been the Determinator.

There is no doubt his father, who seemed to see so much on a racetrack, saw it, too. Dale would later say that he missed his father every day.

One of Dale's favorite stories came up from perhaps the only time father and son raced together. A few circumstances led Dale and a few other minor-leaguers to the Sportsman Division once. Ralph was leading the race. Dale was trying to keep up, concentrating on beating one specific driver.

"With a few laps to go, I see Daddy come up behind me. He's lapping me. I move over to let him pass, but Daddy moves with me. He comes up on my bumper! He starts pushing me! He pushes me past the other guy! Daddy wins! I finish third. The other guy, fourth, is so mad, complaining everywhere about 'those Earnhardts,' but there's nothing he can do. It's over."[4]

Losing him wasn't easy. "It was a heck of a deal," is about as deep as he went publicly.[5]

In talking about his private life, he and his father were similar. In terms of style on the track, Dale

> **QUOTABLE**
>
> "I started racing full time, and that's when I started starving to death."
>
> — Dale Earnhardt

Like Dale Sr.'s early years with his father, Dale Jr. spent many days in the garage working alongside his dad.

drove a different brand of race. Winning was the most important thing. There was a fire in him to wrestle with life's challenges and to confront them and take them down.

Ralph helped give Dale both the work ethic and racing instincts to do just that. Ralph may not have suggested it, but it was there in his son's genes.

"Daddy had begun to help me with engine work and giving me used tires, and he'd talked to Mama about putting me in his car," Dale would say later. "Then he died. It left me in a situation where I had to make it on my own. I'd give up everything I got if he were still alive, but I don't think I'd be where I am if he hadn't died."[6]

From the outset, he drove hard. Maybe too hard. If racing were hockey, Dale would spend most nights in the penalty box for elbowing. That was his way. It was what he felt he needed to do. Being unchained from his dad and left to help provide for his family became driving forces.

DOING IT HIS WAY

If racing were hockey, Dale would spend most nights in the penalty box for elbowing. That was his way. It was what he felt he needed to do.

"It was the biggest shock of my life," he would later say. "I didn't know which way to turn, what to do, where to go for help and advice. I was helpless."[7]

But not on the track. Dale wasn't afraid to bump with cars. He wasn't afraid to dent a few fenders on his way to the front of a pack.

It was working, too. Even before his father died, Dale won races. By 1974, he was generally known as an ornery cat on the short tracks of the South.

Metrolina Speedway was a popular spot, as was the half-mile track in Concord, North Carolina.

A track in Hickory, North Carolina, also saw a lot of racers.

Dale's first race came in a car of his brother-in-law's. Dale was in his late teens. After that race, Dale went looking for ride after ride after ride.

The sands were always shifting under the feet of drivers back then. Sometimes you had a ride, and sometimes you didn't. For a long while, it was no different for Dale Earnhardt. Especially in the beginning.

Without organized standings or national schedules, racing was still very much local. Locals went to their local track and cheered on the drivers, who were also often locals.

It wasn't as if owners were scouting drivers from the smaller divisions and trying to groom them for a "Cup" ride. Because of that, the idea of an "established race team" in the minors was almost absurd in 1974.

Dale fought to keep solid footing in the shifting sands. He jumped at his opportunities and drove as if he wanted to stay.

"I think you work better in debt, or when you're trying to achieve something," he said. "If you don't go out to achieve things, you'll never succeed. You'll never get any further than, 'OK, I've gotta go to work at eight, and I'm getting off at five. Ho-hum.'"[1]

Dale was never much for that kind of life.

There are a number of big-break moments in every career, and Dale started to see the small-but-important ones around 1974. He was still broke and living almost day-to-day.

"We lived in several different places," he said. "We rented a house trailer here and there and had an apartment here and there. Finally, we bought a trailer and set it up beside the shop behind my mother's house, where I kept the race car."[2]

The Earnhardts were growing. Their direction was entirely at the mercy of those shifting sands.

DRIVING DREAMS

Dale wasn't around often. It was almost as if he was living two lives. He took on so much at a young age

Earnhardt's driving career brought with it many long days, and extended stretches of being away from home.

without understanding the consequences. It was probably too much considering his driving dreams.

"A regular guy with a highly irregular desire to outrun everyone and everything," Ken Willis wrote in a description of Dale for the *Daytona Beach News-Journal.*[3]

Racing dominated Dale's life at the expense of all other details. In some ways, if it wasn't a racing detail, it wasn't a detail. It was in 1974 when the attention to racing details started paying off.

Moving away from the red-clay tracks, Earnhardt took his freewheeling, open-throttle show more often to the Sportsman Division. He bought a car from driver Harry Gant and set out to make a name for himself.

"There seemed to be races everywhere, so many that a driver could pick and choose where he'd have his best shot," Montville wrote. "There was Savannah, Georgia, on Thursday nights; a choice between Asheville and Richmond on Friday; South Boston, Virginia, or Hickory or Myrtle Beach on Saturday; Merriville, Tennessee, on Sunday. . . . Home late every night. On the road every day. Sleep was Monday and Tuesday."[4]

Long hours were nothing to Dale. He had worked a couple of eighty-hour weeks at a gas station when he was younger, and he toiled for eight straight days as a welder during the Christmas holidays in the mid-1970s.

From his first days of driving the hulking mid-1950s

TOUGH GOING
Many of Earnhardt's early races weren't unlike his side jobs— dead-enders.

QUOTABLE
"I think you work better in debt, or when you're trying to achieve something."

— Dale Earnhardt

Chevys, Earnhardt wasn't going to be someone who let chance pass him by. He hustled, that's for sure.

CHILDRESS IMPRESSED

A man who would soon become significant in Earnhardt's life took note of the effort. It was Richard Childress. He said Earnhardt improved "by going out and running every little short track in the county. He'd race every opportunity he got, and that's how you get to be good in this sport. Dale always had a lot of natural ability, but he tuned it over the years."[5]

Those races were nothing but a wild night out for some and a raw, formless dream for a kid from Kannapolis.

Growing up and still living in town showed Earnhardt that hard work was a part of everything. Working hard was just about the only way he knew how to live.

In 1975, the Earnhardt name made its first blip on the big-league radar screen. In those days, the current NASCAR "Cup" circuit was called the Grand National division.

"Typical was one Friday-night dirt-track duel for third place . . ." Ed Hinton wrote in a 1995 newspaper article of an incident involving a driver named Stick Elliott. "'Going into the last lap,' Earnhardt said, 'I got right up on old Stick's bumper and caught hold of him just right and spun him around just as pretty as you'll ever see."[6]

Earnhardt developed a reputation as a bit of a dangerous driver. He earned it. Then he'd fan the flames. It was a cycle feeding the frenzy that would become the legend.

"They ain't ever seen the kind of rough racing I've had to do in my life just to survive," Earnhardt said in that 1995 *Sports Illustrated* article. "They don't want to mess with this ol' boy."[7]

Earnhardt so often crystallized thought in speech. There may have been some acting involved, but the brash and confident side of his soul was the one the people saw and loved.

DID YOU KNOW?

In his first nine NASCAR starts, Earnhardt finished in the top five only once.

On May 25, 1975, his break came in NASCAR's longest race. It would last 600 miles. The track, Charlotte Motor Speedway, wasn't far from home.

The competition was strong and well-financed. In fact, it might have been impossible for Earnhardt to win against the famous drivers of the day.

Among the big-time names then, Richard Petty won the race, followed by Cale Yarborough and David Pearson. Earnhardt finished twenty-second in a No. 8 car owned by a man named Ed Negre. Negre finished thirty-second in the race. Earnhardt made $1,925 for his finish.

The driver who finished just behind him was Richard Childress. Earnhardt and Childress became more acquainted and friendly. Childress saw the same potential everyone else saw. Looking back, maybe he saw more potential than most.

"I knew right then that he had everything it was gonna take to be somebody," Childress said.[8]

RIDING THE TOP CIRCUIT

Over the next few seasons, Earnhardt raced on the top circuit when he was given a ride. Mostly, he was back in the Sportsman Division. He cashed his checks for a couple hundred bucks a shot, pinched his pennies, and waited for The Show to come calling again.

He raced twice in the big leagues in 1976. He raced there one time in 1977. In 1978, he caught an even bigger break from a man named Roy Osterlund.

In one of his earliest interviews with the Grand National press, he admitted his ambitions for the country's bicentennial.

"Who knows what a good showing might mean?" he said in

TRACK FACT

Earnhardt's first start came in the longest race of the NASCAR season (600 miles) and took place at the track closest to Kannapolis.

Cale Yarborough was among NASCAR's top drivers when Earnhardt broke into the circuit.

1976. "Assurance of a future ride in some more big races at best. . . . I'm hepped up about the chance, no sense denying that."[9]

Unfortunately, even his semi-promising offers seemed to go up in smoke. Earnhardt made his third Grand National appearance as an injury replacement for an owner and driver named Johnny Ray. That was at the Dixie 500 on November 7, 1976.

He ended up in a horrific wreck. Earnhardt couldn't remember flipping the car after the race. What he couldn't forget were his circumstances.

"It was just a one-race deal," he said, "but it might have been much more if I hadn't torn up the car. Man, that's all Johnny Ray has is that car."[10]

His part-time rides weren't in very good cars, but a handful of Grand National races in 1978 led to the start of something big.

Enter Osterlund. He had money, and he wanted to fund a race team to compete with the big boys. As Osterlund was getting involved, he had some novel ideas. Among them: doing his homework and scouting for a talented driver.

Earnhardt's name came up. It always did when someone started talking about a guy to fill a seat.

That was Earnhardt. He was in the running to be in the running, so to speak. With all he had gone

QUOTABLE

"Hampton, Ga. — Dale Earnhardt, a promising young driver from Kannapolis, flipped and turned an immaculate Chevy racer into a mass of crushed metal Sunday, but walked away with only a slightly cut hand."

— The *Charlotte Observer*, November 8, 1976

through, he was an easy guy to root for. Osterlund gave him a shot at the November 1978 race in Atlanta. He started tenth and drove the No. 98 car to a fourth-place finish. His winnings were $6,900. It was the highest finish in his nine big-league starts.

Earnhardt made quite a name for himself that day. With all the twists and turns in his life, the wrong ways and the dead-end jobs, it seemed Earnhardt had set the racing wheel straight. He found a career groove on the track on that day.

In 1979, with Osterlund backing him all season, Earnhardt began his assault on the record books.

TRACK FACT

In 1978, Earnhardt earned more than $20,000 in five races.

For a guy who couldn't find steady work a few short years prior, Earnhardt's luck was changing.

During the 1978 audition, Earnhardt was driving a second car that Osterlund had entered in Atlanta. In 1979, Earnhardt went from moonlighting to headlining for the California businessman.

Osterlund's main driver, Dave Marcis, left the team before the 1979 season. Finally, a seat was open for the twenty-seven year old with the untamed hair and a reputation to match.

Earnhardt quickly made his impression, often on drivers' doors and fenders, and he made good on a Humpy Wheeler prediction.

STARDOM PREDICTED

"It's been a long time since I've seen a youngster so determined, so hungry," Wheeler told the *Charlotte Observer* in 1976. "If nothing happens to sour his attitude, I think he's going to be a star within a few years—a big one."[1]

Those "few years" had passed. Earnhardt had set his course and he let fly for stardom.

In addition to a seat, Osterlund put his driver in a house on Lake Norman in North Carolina. Like the sensibilities of its new occupant, the house wasn't far from Kannapolis. Osterlund provided funding, support, structure, and some stability.

"I never had a lot of money to worry about or invest and Rod tried to help me do that," Earnhardt said later. "He wanted me to invest wisely and things like that. None of it worked out then, but I had a regular paycheck with my salary and other things. It was a much better situation."[2]

Earnhardt started tearing up the tracks, just as he'd always dreamed. Rather than scraping for a ride and chasing paychecks across the South, Earnhardt had a schedule. It was national, more organized, and

BIG YEAR
In 1979,
Earnhardt
went from
moonlighting
to headlining.

more complicated in some ways. He raced on huge superspeedways. There were also road courses that required turning left and right. And there were short tracks. That's where the high-banked, half-mile track of Bristol Motor Speedway fits into the story.

On April 1, 1979, Earnhardt won his first Grand National race there in Bristol, Tennessee. The name of the race was the Southeastern 500, and Earnhardt became the first rookie in two years to win on the circuit.

It seemed only natural that a story as improbable as Earnhardt's found its first great professional accomplishment on April Fool's Day. The winner's take was nearly $20,000.

Earnhardt beat pros such as Bobby Allison, Darrell Waltrip, Richard Petty, Benny Parsons, Childress, Marcis, and Gant for his first win.

"I'll probably believe it in the morning," Earnhardt said after the race. "This is a bigger thrill than my first-ever racing victory. This was a win in the big leagues, against top-caliber drivers. It wasn't at some dirt track back at home."[3]

In 1979, Earnhardt began to make his mark by winning his first Grand National race.

Earnhardt credited his crew for the win. That became a ritual, and was something he'd be doing for the rest of his career. He also thanked some of the legends he beat for treating him well. That was the thing about Earnhardt. He raced hard, he raced to win, and he was human.

Earnhardt's crew returned the praise back to him. Crew chief Jake Elder agreed that the car had performed well, but credited Earnhardt's skill for the win.

Earnhardt went on to win four poles in 1979, and

QUOTABLE
"This is a bigger thrill than my first-ever racing victory."

— Earnhardt on his first big-league win

he finished among the top five eleven times. The 1979 season wasn't without its struggles. Not many Earnhardt stories make it all the way around the track without scratching the paint or denting a fender.

"With Earnhardt," said Darrell Waltrip, a frequent rival in those years, "every lap is a controlled crash."[4] The two had their share of run-ins while Earnhardt was on the rise. In terms of wrecks people remember, Earnhardt already had suffered a major one—the 1976 crash in a borrowed car. Trouble came knocking on his door again on July 30, 1979, at Pocono.

TRACK FACT

In Earnhardt's first full season, 1979, he won a staggering $237,575.

The historical archive reads, simply, "Accident." It doesn't begin to tell the damage. He hit the wall hard.

"When the car finally stopped, he was stuffed into a helicopter and hurried to East Stroudsburg Hospital, where he was treated for two broken collarbones, a concussion, and severe bruises of the neck and chest," Montville wrote.[5]

Earnhardt didn't race again until September 9 of that year. He missed four races and dropped from fifth in the standings to twelfth. Still, he managed to claw his way back to seventh overall.

ROOKIE HONORS

The rookie had a great team. He publicly thanked them for almost every good turn he made. The combination pushed Earnhardt to the Rookie of the Year award, with winnings of $237,575 in 1979. In racing circles, he earned respect, rivalries, and expectations heading into 1980.

The Osterlund team was primed for 1980. They were determined to avoid a sophomore slump.

"Even missing four races in 1979, I still finished seventh in points," Earnhardt said. "I felt good about that. The car was competitive and finished races. If we could do that again in 1980, we had a real good shot at the championship."[6]

Earnhardt was even better in 1980. Much better. The best, in fact. In the first race of the season, he finished second. He followed that by taking fourth place in the second race, which was the Daytona 500. He took over the points lead.

Earnhardt had reached the pinnacle of stock car racing. Earnhardt put his hard-charging car out front early in 1980.

SETTING A BENCHMARK

No one before Earnhardt had ever won a championship in his second NASCAR season.

Then he stood hard on the pedal and kept the field in his rear-view mirror the rest of the way. At last, Earnhardt was the champion of NASCAR's top circuit. Even his son, Dale Jr., looks back at a legend in the making.

"He was awesome and fearless in those days— it seemed like he would win or crash trying," he said.[7]

Winning as a sophomore was unheard of. Earnhardt won five races in all, and finished among the top five in 19 of 31 races.

SETTING HIGH STANDARDS

Earnhardt was a form of history on wheels.

While it wasn't necessary, Osterlund's team could have been even more dominant in 1980. Earnhardt's cars ran into engine trouble in some qualifying races and had four separate "Engine Failure" finishes.[8]

"I'll tell you what makes that car run. Dale Earnhardt makes that car run," said one NASCAR crew chief.[9] His point was that Earnhardt could make the most out of his car.

With skill and "touch," Earnhardt nearly doubled his 1979 winnings. His exposure also hit new heights.

On August 4, 1980, the *New York Times* profiled him. The kid from Kannapolis? Profiled by the *New*

Team owner Richard Childress (left) saw Earnhardt's potential early in his career.

York Times? Earnhardt came off well, too. He was painted hanging out with his friends: "This is Earnhardt at his best, sitting around with just plain folks and reminiscing about the good old times."[10]

The newspaper story even mentioned "two deliciously sassy and bright children"—Kelley and Dale Jr.—and their dad making trips to see them after Earnhardt and their mom divorced.[11]

Racing was even more compelling because it paid for Earnhardt's lake house, a boat with all the

options, the sports car, and a freedom from the chains of debt and go-nowhere jobs. Aside from the stresses of loosened family ties, 1980 was a very good year for Earnhardt. The following season was not.

The hot-shot Rookie of the Year from 1979, who won the whole deal in 1980, did not win in 1981. In addition, he was about to be blindsided by news he couldn't control. Bad news. Osterlund sold the successful race team . . . during the season.

DID YOU KNOW?

Earnhardt finished in the top five a combined thirty times between the 1979 and 1980 seasons.

The dream team of Childress and Earnhardt wasn't quite ready for prime time. If timing is everything, the pair needed a few more years honing their skills separately before taking over the stock car world together in 1984.

As an owner in 1981, Childress wasn't prepared to take on NASCAR with one of the best stock car drivers in the world. He felt that Earnhardt's racing style might end up costing too much money.

After the twentieth race of the 1981 season, Earnhardt drove the

Earnhardt's wife, Teresa, shown with Dale Jr. in 2002, started building the Earnhardt franchise in 1982.

No. 3 for Childress. He was just warming the seat. His finishes were better than average, but Childress had much more than average on his mind.

Childress thought ahead, and he thought big. It takes an honest adult to make the kind of assessment that followed. At the end of the 1981 season, Childress let Earnhardt go.

LOOKING FOR A RIDE

"I just wasn't ready to carry him," Childress said. "I knew that Dale had the ability to go on, and I wanted him to do that."[1]

Like Earnhardt, Childress was very ambitious. Unfortunately, while a driver just needs a break, an owner needs cash—especially with Earnhardt. The hair-raising driver stuck his car's nose in all sorts of places it wasn't exactly meant to go. Through almost every turn, Earnhardt was brutal on his cars.

"We talked about staying together in 1982, but we didn't feel there would be enough money on hand to build the team we needed," Dale said. "It was going to take more time."[2]

Childress went to work catching up to Earnhardt's heavy foot. At that time, maybe no one was running equipment tough enough for Dale Earnhardt. The next owner who learned this the hard way was Bud Moore. He gave Earnhardt his 1982 and 1983 rides. That's when Earnhardt drove a yellow-and-blue No. 15 car.

BRIEF PARTING

After parting ways briefly after the 1981 season, Childress went to work catching up to Earnhardt's heavy foot.

By the 1982 season, Earnhardt had lost some pace on the extraordinary momentum from 1979 and 1980. In those two seasons, he was a young and hungry freight train. His Osterlund team made that car sing, and Earnhardt made it dance.

Entering 1982, he was just another driver on a losing streak. The NASCAR field was full of those guys. Not many, though, were making headlines for what they had not done lately.

A 2001 *Atlanta Journal-Constitution* story looked back at an *Atlanta Journal* headline from the early part of the 1982 season. "Dale Earnhardt: From the heights to faded glory," it read.[3]

It took six races, but Earnhardt found his way back to Victory Lane on April 4, 1982, in Darlington, South Carolina. The former champion didn't pick up another win until July 16, 1983.

Earnhardt won once more for Bud Moore on July 31, 1983, at the Talladega 500. Overall, success didn't happen for Earnhardt in the No. 15 car.

Since the dream season of 1980, Earnhardt had his share of trouble. There was the winless 1981 split between three owners (he finished seventh overall).

DID YOU KNOW?

When driving for Childress, Earnhardt piloted a No. 3 car. With owner Bud Moore, he was in a No. 15.

There was the one win 1982 for Bud Moore (he finished twelfth overall). And Earnhardt finished eighth after the two-win 1983 season.

TROUBLED TIMES

His union with Moore was plagued by equipment problems. During the 1982 and 1983 seasons, Earnhardt's cars went down with about a dozen engine failures, and had problems with a number of other key parts that caused him to leave races: head gasket, clutch, brake stud, brakes, steering, battery, oil leak, ball joint, heating, and overheating.

"What hurt Bud, me and the team during the 1982 season, for example, was the car breaking and all," Earnhardt said later. "It's hard to come back after you've fallen out of, say, 10 straight races."[4]

For Earnhardt, the early 1980s meant four different owners and only three wins on the track. Off the track, his life was going the other way. Earnhardt's house was filling up. As usual, the details aren't all sunshine and clean air.

It took a devastating 1981 fire in his second wife's home to reunite Earnhardt with Dale Jr. and Kelley under one roof.

Brenda was forced to move nearer to her family in Virginia. Dale Jr. had lived with his father only three of his first six years. Kelley was eight years old at the time. While their father courted superstardom, times could be hard on them. Dale Jr. and Kelley became a team of their own over the years.

Earnhardt, meanwhile, remarried in 1982. His third wife's name was Teresa Houston. She was also from a North Carolina racing family. In the following years, she was as important to the Earnhardt legend and its legacy as anyone. In some ways, she was even more important.

"When he talks about his wife," Sam Moses wrote for *Sports Illustrated* in 1987, " . . . he often brags about her brains, beauty and accomplishments, and especially the fact that she got through high school in two years."[5]

With her business abilities, Teresa helped Earnhardt move from a legendary race car driver to a legendary brand. They formed a company named Dale Earnhardt Inc.

A COMPANY IS BORN

"DEI" eventually outgrew its first home office. It wound up in a huge, gorgeous, glassed-in palace of cars and race shops and offices and a tribute that celebrated and housed their operation. It was so large in scale and scope that many called it the Garage Mahal. That would come after they'd been together for a

Dale's third wife, Teresa, also came from a North Carolina-based racing family.

little while. At first, the marriage process started in true Earnhardt fashion.

He proposed from a hospital bed after breaking his leg in 1982 at Pocono. The wreck was another nasty one. Earnhardt's No. 15 car slammed the wall and took off—on its side. The car nearly jumped the retaining wall as it caught air. The car leaned over, slid upside down on its trunk, then its hood, until it came to a merciful stop.

Earnhardt walked away—skipped, really, with a limp on one leg—down the racetrack and into a waiting ambulance.

Even the television announcers covering the event were fooled by Earnhardt's skip. They commented that it appeared he was bruised but appeared to be fine.

Earnhardt raced the next week.

Meanwhile, Ricky Rudd was running just fine with Childress in the No. 3 car. In fact, he won two races for Childress between 1982 and 1983. Childress still had more than "just fine" in mind, and he knew a driver with a limitless bag of tricks, too—Dale Earnhardt.

For the 1984 season, Earnhardt climbed back into the No. 3 and made his way toward unheard of fame and fortune. The company known as RCR (Richard Childress Racing) would become the most progressive stock car team in the land.

Race victories were straight ahead. Championships were around the corner. Luxury hotels, RVs, yachts, helicopters, and jet planes were down the road. Race teams and the kind of wealth that can float a few generations of dreams were on the horizon.

Earnhardt's ride would go on to surpass the average American Dream. In fact, the level of success that Earnhardt found would seem more like an impossible dream.

It started for Earnhardt and Childress in 1984 at the Talladega 500. Earnhardt hadn't won since the same race the previous year. No one had ever won there back-to-back, let alone with a new make of car and a new owner.

But this was Earnhardt. He won in a fantastic finish. Earnhardt, sitting behind Terry Labonte, was

Crashes like this one in 1982 left Earnhardt with a broken leg and in need of a new car to race.

waiting and waiting. On the last lap, Earnhardt, the avid hunter who could wait and stalk with the best of them, shot into action. His car darted to the front and he held on for a close, tense, and compelling finish.

"It was the most exciting race I've ever been involved with here," Earnhardt said in a post-race report. "It seemed I

TRACK FACT
During the 1982 and 1983 seasons, Earnhardt finished only fifteen races in the top five.

was always wondering what to do while everyone else was doing something. There were 10 or 12 cars always racing for the lead."[6]

There were a total of sixty-eight lead changes. After more than three hours and twelve miunutes of racing, Earnhardt's margin of victory wasn't even two seconds. It was exciting on its own, and it was exciting for what it set in motion.

"You cherish all your wins," Earnhardt said in a post-race interview. "I'll cherish the victory here last year because it was my last with Bud and I'll cherish this one because it is my first with Richard and Chevrolet."[7]

The *Charlotte Observer*'s Tom Higgins wrote the race "could rank as motorsports' greatest race."[8]

With top-ten finishes in sixteen of the 1984 season's first nineteen races, Earnhardt added to his overall points lead.

A couple of poor starts down the stretch slipped Earnhardt out of the top spot. He finished fourth overall in 1984 with two race wins. Earlier in the season, Earnhardt told the *Charlotte Observer* he felt as if it was the start of a beautiful relationship.

THE NO. 3
From 1984 until the end of his career, Earnhardt's big-league ride was in the No. 3.

OPTIMISM REIGNS

"I don't think there has been a time in my career when I've felt any better about a situation or been any more optimistic than I am now," he said.[9]

In 1985, his average finish fell from 9.6 to 14.6, but he won four races. In the first paragraph in each of his four Earnhardt-win race recaps, writer Steve Waid used the words "bold," "rugged," "aggressive, daredevil" and "gutsy."[10]

With Earnhardt driving and the Childress team working on ways to make Earnhardt more consistent, they were on the verge of dominating.

Montville said the goal of the Childress operation was to put "a fearless driver in an unbreakable car."[11]

After bouncing around the No. 8, 30, 77, 19, and 96 cars through 1979, and after longer stints in the No. 2 and the 15, Earnhardt settled for good in the No. 3. It was an enviable position for Earnhardt in the coming years.

QUOTABLE

"I don't think there has been a time in my career when I've felt any better about a situation or been any more optimistic than I am now."

— Dale Earnhardt

Dale Earnhardt (in car No. 3) works his way through the pack during a race in 1985.

They would have the strongest equipment. They would have the strongest program. They would have the strongest cars. They would have the strongest driver. If those elements lined up, it was almost unfair.

The elements lined up in 1986 and 1987.

Over the next decade, so much about NASCAR would change dramatically. The cars changed. The sponsors changed. Media coverage changed. Teams changed. The drivers changed. The money changed.

With each new season, NASCAR smoked the tires at Daytona, slammed the machine into gear, and sped into the season. Along the way, the sport kept gaining popularity. It quickly grew from a regional sport to a national phenomenon.

Remarkably, even Earnhardt changed . . . eventually.

Through it all, he won. And won. And then he won some more. The hot streak began in 1986.

It was from his familiar seat in that No. 3 car—body angled toward the driver's-side window, eyes peering through his bubble goggles—that Earnhardt made himself part of NASCAR's powerful engine.

THE DOMINATOR

Somewhere, though, deep down, the game was still about going fast. No one did that better from the mid-'80s to mid-'90s than Dale Earnhardt.

In 1986, he took a giant leap into the most professionally rewarding career NASCAR had seen to that point.

Six different drivers won in the first six races in '86. That streak ended when Earnhardt backed up an April 13 win with another victory on April 20.

"Dale got the lead and I really overdrove it in the corners, hoping to get close to him and maybe give him a little 'Dale Earnhardt' in the rear bumper. But I couldn't do it," said Ricky Rudd, who

THANK YOU
After winning his second overall championship, Earnhardt was quick to thank his car owner and crew in 1986.

Earnhardt's trophy collection blossomed in 1986, when he won his second NASCAR points title.

finished second to Earnhardt on April 20.[1] The field chased Earnhardt almost the rest of the way. On May 4, 1986, he took over the points lead and never looked back.

A few of his competitors wanted to look back, however. Especially Darrell Waltrip. Later in life, they'd grow much closer as two old buddies with a long history and a shared passion. But in the 1980s, it was a full-on rivalry.

Waltrip spoke for the drivers who saw Earnhardt as a bully. Some accused Earnhardt of bumping leaders out of the way to finish first. In fact, NASCAR fined Earnhardt for a February 1986 incident that involved Waltrip. If it were a footrace, and a second-place runner tripped the first-place runner, that would be poor sportsmanship. Earnhardt didn't think of driving cars as a footrace.

Thanks to his driving—and his team of Childress and crew chief Kirk Shelmerdine—Earnhardt finished first in 1986. He thanked the man he considered most responsible.

"It was Richard's [Childress] effort that built the team and put it in the position it is in today. Anytime you run an entire season without a lot of loose ends to tie, you have confidence and you know you are going to do well."[2]

LOVE HIM OR HATE HIM

Through his own success, Earnhardt became polarizing. Some drivers were OK with his style, and some guys weren't. Some fans loved his driving, and some fans hated it. Either way, they were interested.

In 1987, sports fans everywhere saw a run like few others. The No. 3 car finished fifth at Daytona. Earnhardt followed that by winning six of the next seven races. He went on to win 11 of the season's 29 races.

Along the way, Earnhardt continued to bang fenders and ruffle feathers. Despite his fine in 1986, he found more incidents in 1987. Critics might say he put himself there on purpose. NASCAR fined him again in 1987. He still finished as clearly the circuit's top driver that year, earning his third Cup title.

"Those were the two great years," Shelmerdine would say. "In '86–'87, we had the best stuff out there. No one could touch us."[3]

TRACK FACT
In 1987, Earnhardt's average finish was 5.9, the highest of his career.

TRACK FACT
Earnhardt passed the $17 million mark in career earnings in 1987.

Following the 1987 season, Childress & Co. changed sponsors. The change put Earnhardt in a black No. 3 car. That's where the nickname "The Man in Black" comes from.

The results weren't as dominating in 1988, 1989, 1990, or 1991, but Earnhardt spent only three weeks over those next four seasons outside of fifth in the overall standings. He also won two more titles.

In 1988, Bill Elliott won six races and took the title. Earnhardt finished third after winning three races.

The next season had its share of disappointing finishes, too. Still, the team almost won another championship. Earnhardt won the final race of the season, but it

DID YOU KNOW?

In 1987, Earnhardt had winning streaks four races in a row, three races in a row, and two races in a row.

REMARKABLE RUN—1987

Race #	Race Name	Finish
2	Goodwrench 500	1
3	Miller High Life 400	1
4	Motorcraft 500	16
5	TransSouth 500	1
6	First Union 400	1
7	Valleydale 500	1
8	Sovran Bank 500	1

wasn't enough to top Rusty Wallace for the 1989 title. Earnhardt congratulated Wallace. He even drew at least one positive review for his driving.

"Dale Earnhardt gave me all the room that I needed to win that race," Mark Martin said after a race in September of 1989. "I just didn't quite have the car to do it."[4]

> QUOTABLE
> **"In '86–'87, we had the best stuff out there. No one could touch us."**
>
> **— Kirk Shelmerdine**

Earnhardt still raced hard, but he grated on fewer nerves as he neared forty. The one-time wild-eyed teen had now been happily married for years. He had become a parent again when Taylor Nicole was born in 1988. By then, he played a role in the lives of all his children.

Around that time, *Racing for Kids* published Kelley's thoughts on growing up as an Earnhardt. There were fewer racing stories and more about sharing time.

BUILDING A BRAND

By the early 1990s, Earnhardt could retire any day he wanted. He had 300 acres in Mooresville, North Carolina. He could travel wherever he wanted to go.

That's the upside of becoming a brand name. Too often, though, people only saw the name.

Behind the mirrored sunglasses straight from an Arnold Schwarzenegger action movie, there resided a Dale Earnhardt known to his family and friends. Behind those glasses was the soul of a driver.

By 1990 Earnhardt had bagged enough race wins to retire as a Hall of Famer. After the winning the season-ending race in 1989, but losing the championship, he pointed to 1990.

"We came up a little short [12 points] of winning the championship," Earnhardt said then. "But I'm already looking forward to 1990 and the Daytona 500. All I need is just a few days off to do some deer hunting and I'll be ready to go."[5]

Earnhardt went out and won nine races in 1990. None of them was the Daytona 500, however. Earnhardt led an amazing 155 of 200 laps in the 1990 season opener only to cut a tire and fall off the pace with less than a mile to go.

"What a heartbreaker," Childress said. "To be a half mile from something you've dreamed about all your life—man, that's awfully hard to take."[6]

Earnhardt recovered to win his sixth overall championship. He won the championship again in 1991. He also won four races overall and chalked up the fiftieth victory of his career that season. Off the

Earnhardt paraded his Winston Cup Series championship around New York City as part of his duties as champion.

track, he was starting to view life from different angles. Rather than wrestling all of it to the ground, he accepted more.

"I'll never do it again," he said in 1991, "but at one time I gave up too much to racing."[7]

Earnhardt never lost the will to win, but he had discovered other passions that took a little of his edge off . . . in a good way.

"I'm not sure about some of this intimidation stuff," he said before the 1991 season. "Maybe that was the case a few years ago when I was wilder. . . .

I think as I've matured more finesse has figured in to go along with the aggression."[8]

Earnhardt's second career attempt at winning three championships in a row didn't materialize. The wheels went wobbly in 1992. Earnhardt won only a single race and wound up twelfth overall. It was his worst finish since the 1982 season. Following the 1992 campaign, Shelmerdine left the team. Andy Petree became the new crew chief in 1993. He made an immediate impact.

"Durability had almost become an obsession with these guys," he said of the Childress approach. "There comes a time when you have to push the envelope."[9]

Earnhardt recorded a pair of second-place finishes at the season's beginning and made a run at his sixth overall championship.

DID YOU KNOW?

Earnhardt's 1992 finish at twelfth overall marked only one of three full seasons in which he finished outside the top nine.

TRACK FACT

Between 1986 and 1991, Earnhardt's lowest overall finish was third.

FIRE STILL BURNS

The fact he was still so competitive tickled him.

"It's pretty neat to be chased," he said after a win on July 3, 1993. "At my stage in my career and feeling as good as I do, it's still neat to be the guy to beat. . . . The fire is still as hot as ever."[10]

Sadly, NASCAR and Earnhardt suffered losses beyond the track in 1993. The 1992 champion, Alan Kulwicki, died in a plane crash in April. Earnhardt friend and NASCAR veteran Davey Allison died in a helicopter crash in July.

After a win that month, Earnhardt took a clockwise victory lap in honor of a Kulwicki move. Earnhardt held a No. 28 flag out in honor of Allison's number.

"I'd have been glad to run second to him today [to] have him back," Earnhardt said. "It's pretty emotional, and tough to describe. There's nothing anybody can say or do—just honor and remember him the best way we can."[11]

After a six-win 1993, Earnhardt won yet another championship. In 1994, Earnhardt tied "The King," Richard Petty, with his seventh championship.

"I still shake my head sometimes when I see what Dale Earnhardt does in a race car," Petree said after one win. "It looked like we were going to get beat today, and then the next thing I know, he's out front again. I don't know how he does it, but he seems to always get the job done."[12]

He completed the season with four wins, seven seconds, and six thirds. There were only six of thirty-one races where he finished outside of the top ten.

In all, it was a remarkable run. The same could be said for the previous decade. He had changed as a driver and as a man. He had drawn even with Petty. And he had earned Petty's respect, too.

"I feel like I had my time in stock car racing, and I helped expand it," Petty said. "Now it's Earnhardt's time to help expand it. Racing needs somebody like Earnhardt to carry the torch on to whoever the next cat is. Dale took it from where I carried it to, and he'll carry it a little bit further, and then somebody's gonna come along and take it even further, hopefully."[13]

RIVALRY BLOOMS

From the time Earnhardt won his first championship through 1994, NASCAR had changed in many ways. Some saw the changes as progress. Others missed the old-school feel of the races.

In NASCAR's early days, sponsors were mostly companies with an interest in racing. They were oil companies, car manufacturers, auto parts companies, or tire makers. Through Earnhardt's run of championships, other sponsors were attracted to the sport. Discount stores, health care products, and other mainstream businesses jumped on board. Media interest grew from handfuls to hordes. The cost of ownership ran well into the millions of dollars.

CONTINUED GROWTH

Some budgets even included accessories such as entire extra race teams—with the additional crew members, mechanics, engineers, engine builders, garage bays, haulers, recreational vehicles, and drivers.

Earnhardt was in the ownership game, too. He drove for his own company as a part-timer in the minor leagues when time allowed. Many drivers raced both the big-league and the minor-league races on some weekends if the circuits shared a track. In the big leagues, he didn't drive for DEI, only Childress.

Earnhardt also supported the racing dreams of Kerry, Kelley, and Dale Jr. All three of them raced in the late-model division with help from a company Earnhardt started called Chance Racing. With growing business needs, their dad and Teresa started building a large and lavish race shop. Fronted by sheets of tall glass, it accounted for hundreds of thousands of square feet. It was among the first of the super shops that have since become the norm.

By the mid-1990s, the racing game was harder to play. It was a big-money game and the small-money

Earnhardt and Jeff Gordon forged one of the memorable rivalries in sports in the 1990s.

players—from tracks to drivers—were endangered. No longer were drivers just good ol' boys from the South with a couple buddies turning lug nuts. Drivers were from the North, from the West, and from the Midwest. Crews were stocked with experts in their fields.

BOY WONDER

The new drivers were younger and more polished. Many came with movie-star looks and movie-star dreams. NASCAR was their Hollywood. Fifteen years after Earnhardt's first *New York Times* profile, the July 16, 1995, edition featured another flattering NASCAR piece on someone called "Wonder Boy."

That was the not-so-flattering nickname Earnhardt dropped on the head of Jeff Gordon. Gordon was named the Rookie of the Year in 1993 and had loads of talent to go with his loads of opportunity.

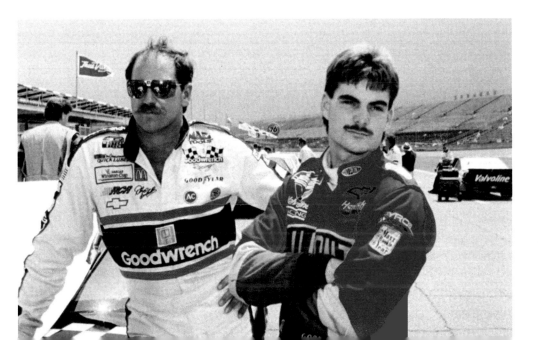

In his second year, Gordon did not win a championship as Earnhardt had, but he did make an impact. Gordon won the first Brickyard 400 at historic Indianapolis Motor Speedway. He also won the 600-mile race that year in Charlotte, Earnhardt's backyard.

At the time of the 1995 story, Gordon and Earnhardt were clanging their way toward the championship. Outwardly, Gordon and Earnhardt couldn't have been more different. Anyone who dug a little deeper found a great deal of mutual respect in the years that followed. But the other angle, on the surface, was much easier to see. It also seemed to draw the most publicity.

DREAM DRIVERS

Younger drivers arrived with movie-star looks and movie-star dreams. NASCAR was their Hollywood.

Contrasting the two was easy. Their differences were striking. Earnhardt was an old-school Southerner with those hard-earned lines in his face. He had a mischievous smile dancing behind his bristle of mustache. He could be short on words, but could drag out his drawl if it suited him.

Gordon was a fresh face with clean-cut looks. He was born in California. He didn't have a drawl, and there weren't any hard-luck stories about driving to put food on the table. It wasn't his fault, of course, but Gordon was made a target early in his career.

The angle: The Man in Black vs. the kid with the colorful paint scheme on his car and the "Rainbow Warriors" in his pit.

A RIVALRY BORN

Earnhardt had rivals before. He talked about those guys, too. But there was something too good about this budding rivalry. Publicly, the cagey legend dropped the anvils when he could. Maybe Earnhardt felt threatened. Maybe he was just having fun. And maybe he knew that a foil made for interesting drama.

Whatever the equation, it seemed to work. NASCAR attendance jumped from around 3 million in 1989 to nearly 5 million in 1994. Fans were watching on television and NASCAR had become one of the fastest-growing sports in the country.

The story of NASCAR's rise in those years can't be told without Gordon. There was something about the kid. Of all the young guns flooding into the sport, he was the best of them. Gordon earned Earnhardt's respect.

The two did wind up battling down the stretch in 1995. Earnhardt held the overall points lead over the first half of the season. Gordon had a strong

Earnhardt won at the Brickyard in 1995, and questions of a rivalry with Jeff Gordon immediately followed.

second half. In his No. 24 car, Gordon won seven races overall. Earnhardt won five, including the second annual Brickyard 400. Post-race interview questions touched on a rivalry.

"I'm not going to take anything away from Jeff, his talents or his team," Earnhardt said. "His future is bright. He's a great racer who is due all the press and the reputation he's got. But there have been a lot of others who have come along before him."[1]

The Brickyard made for another proud feather in Earnhardt's cap. He nearly won his eighth title, too. Four consecutive top-two finishes in the middle of the season put Gordon in front. Earnhardt kept on his bumper in the standings. In fact, the 1995 points race came down to the last race of the season. Earnhardt won the race by almost four seconds, but points leader Gordon finished thirty-second to clinch the overall championship. "Wonder Boy" won his first title.

The veteran graciously congratulated Gordon's owner, Rick Hendrick. For his efforts, Gordon chalked up more than $2 million in earnings from his races.

In 1996, Gordon finished the overall points race in second

behind Hendrick teammate Terry Labonte. In 1997, Gordon won another championship.

DOWN YEARS

The track wasn't kind to Earnhardt over those two seasons from 1996–97. He signed a new contract with Childress after the 1995 season, then won the pole for the 1996 season-opener at Daytona. He wound up finishing second to Dale Jarrett. It was yet another close-but-not-quite finish at Daytona.

Earnhardt recovered and was in first overall after the eight races of the 1996

TRACK FACT
Earnhardt won five races in 1995, slipped to two wins in 1996, and did not win a race in 1997. Still, he finished second, fourth, and fifth in the standings.

season. Eight races later, he had conceded the lead. Two weeks after that, a frightening crash disrupted the whole run.

On July 28, 1996, while leading the race, he kicked out of the pack and headed immediately for the wall at Talladega's superspeedway. The wreck was violent and left his car looking like someone had taken a bite out of it. To watch is to remember how fast things

A DOWNTURN

Earnhardt had fallen off the pace from his championship average finishes in the 8.0 area in 1993 and 1994, to 9.2 in 1995, 11.1 in 1996, and 12.1 in 1997.

happen at nearly 200 m.p.h. It takes one car involved in a wreck nearly fifteen seconds of skidding before it comes to a peaceful stop.

The No. 3 wasn't so lucky that day at Talladega. Earnhardt was left with a broken sternum and collar bone. Once he was cut out of the car, he walked to a nearby ambulance. He even managed to give the thumbs-up to the crowd.

Then he went out and started the next race. He drove the first five laps of the Brickyard 400. Then he gave way to a relief driver. Not finishing the race seemed to hurt Earnhardt more than the injuries.

"It's hard to get out of there," he said after the swap. "It's my life."[2]

In 1997, he reflected on the image he portrayed that day. "I think that made people see I'm human, that I know how it feels to hurt. I don't mean from the injury, I mean from the heart. I'm not embarrassed by what happened. It's the way I felt. You didn't see one-tenth of how I was really feeling inside and just how close I came to bawling like a baby."[3]

Earnhardt, however, didn't lose sight of another championship in his mind. Winning No. 8 would be special and historic.

After the Brickyard, he managed to qualify first in the following race on a road course. Then he went out and ran the ninety-lap race without relief. That meant nearly 1,000 turns with two upper-body fractures.

The legend grew that day. Too bad championships aren't won on courage alone. He finished fourth in the overall points standings at the end of the 1996 season.

The next season, 1997, was a winless one. It was the first time he had gone an entire season without a win since 1981. On top of that, the season started out ugly. An accident at Daytona caused a poor finish. Gordon, for his part, finished first and was followed by two more Hendrick cars in a 1-2-3 owner sweep.

Earnhardt never blamed his 1996 injury, but racing couldn't have been easy for a guy getting bounced around in a cramped cockpit at more than forty-five years old.

When he could, he continued to spend time away from the track. He had the helicopters and jets. He had taken in tens of millions of dollars. He had a working farm with chickens and horses and cattle and deer and fish in its ponds.

When he chose, he could move the earth with his choice of big toys—bulldozer or backhoe or tractor. He could fish in his back yard or hunt in Canada, or the other way around.

And, there was more tragedy at the track. One of Earnhardt's favorite travel companions, Neil Bonnett, died in a 1994 racing accident at Daytona.

He had the makings of a guy winding down his racing career. Maybe he was ready to ease out of the No. 3 seat and leave the racing to the younger drivers.

As the 1998 season dawned, there were whispers about Earnhardt's abilities being in decline. Earnhardt responded by opening the 1998 season with a statement for the rest of the racing world—he was still a force.

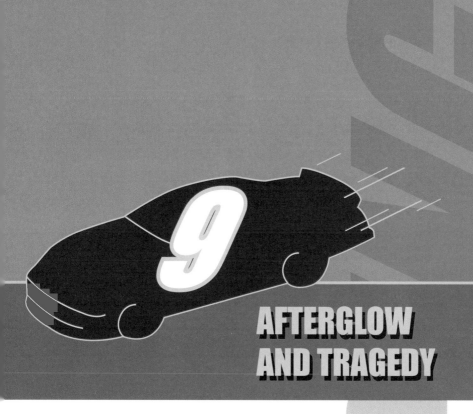

AFTERGLOW AND TRAGEDY

Earnhardt had become the Daytona 500's sympathetic character over the years. Only one race had ever brought him down in a fight. It just happened to be the biggest one on the calendar.

If sports fans still believe in what should happen, well, Earnhardt should win the Daytona 500. He had to, right?

His failures were well-documented. Even his achievements were somehow not good enough. Second place three times from 1993–97 still meant he was losing. After the Talladega crash in 1996, fans and media felt they were watching the setting sun.

"The crash at Talladega was about the worst crash you can imagine without someone getting killed," Humpy Wheeler said.[1]

Then Earnhardt wrecked at the Daytona 500 in 1997 and went winless the rest of the way. He even blacked out briefly during a race in June that season. After the wreck at Daytona, Earnhardt wasn't all that hurt. He climbed out under his own power. As he was making his way to an ambulance, a light bulb went off in his head.

'I'VE GOT TO GO'

Then came a vintage line from his vintage years.

"I looked over there and said, 'Man, the wheels ain't knocked off that car yet.' I went over there, looked at the wheels and told the guy in the car to fire it up.

"It fired up, I told the guy to get out, then told the ambulance guy to unhook me. I've got to go."[2]

One year later, he went out and won the Daytona 500. Finally.

Few races had ever been more talked about. The achievement probably saw more sports pages than anything else he'd ever done. Earnhardt's doomed Daytona experience finally turned itself around.

Afterward, there wasn't anyone who could wipe the smile off his face.

Many top sports figures have great careers but take years to break through in their sports' biggest events. It took Phil Mickelson years before he finally won his first major golf tournament. John Elway of the Denver Broncos was near the end of his career before he finally won the Super Bowl. For Earnhardt, winning the Daytona 500 was even better. He had come from so far down before reaching the pinnacle of his sport. Still, he wanted more.

In true Earnhardt fashion, he saw more wins at the next turn. He still felt competitive. He did just win at Daytona, after all. Maybe 1998 was the year he'd win his eighth championship.

Even with the wind finally at his back, the momentum faded and Earnhardt fell out of the top ten by the season's midpoint. Things weren't all bad at the track, though. Overall, life was suiting Earnhardt well. As an owner, his career was taking off, thanks in large part to his namesake.

For the first time ever, DEI ran a car in the big leagues in 1998. That left an open seat at DEI's top minor league affiliate.

QUOTABLE

"I told the guy to get out, then told the ambulance guy to unhook me. I've got to go."

— Dale Earnhardt

Dale Jr. had worked his way through a late-model driving career throughout the 1990s. By 1998, he had taken over DEI's ride in NASCAR's top minor league. Father and son often raced at the same tracks on different days.

On the minor league circuit, Dale Jr. was the main attraction. He brought the most fans, the most media, and the most attention. People wanted to see if Earnhardt's kid could drive. Could he ever.

A WIN FOR THE KID

On April 5, 1998, Dale Jr. won his first race. His win at Texas Motor Speedway brought his father to tears for the second time in a year. Before that, Earnhardt wasn't quite sure what to make of his kids' tastes for racing.

"Dale Jr. is making progress. Kerry and Kelley have had some disappointing runs this year. It's there for them if they want to do it," he said. "They've got to start showing some progress or it's going to be hard to keep doing it. They've all got their education and got jobs and they're doing well. If they want to race, they need to focus on it a little more and make it positive."[3]

"Junior" made it more than positive. In June of 1997, his father finally signed the twenty-three-year-old to a proper contract. It was a five-year deal with an option for another five, which would become very important at the end of 2007. Until that point, Earnhardt had given his kid $500 per week and a cut of any winnings. Prior to his racing career taking off, Dale Jr. had worked at his father's car dealership.

The Earnhardt family may have been wealthy, but Dale Sr. didn't feed his kids with silver spoons. In fact, growing up as an Earnhardt was not as easy as it might sound. Dale Jr. attended a military academy for part of his schooling. And before that, as Dale Jr. tells it in *Driver #8*, "He was so focused in winning that even when he was home between races, his mind was still at the racetrack instead of home with us."[4]

Another anecdote from a *Sports Illustrated* article drew

DID YOU KNOW?

Earnhardt raced with a lucky penny stuck to his dashboard during the 1998 Daytona 500. It was given to him by a nine-year-old girl he met through the Make-A-Wish foundation.

on the same theme. "Sometimes he'd come back home from somewhere in the country, after he won a race, and he'd get on another plane to go hunting somewhere."[5]

"Little E" came to understand his father's commitment. In fact, the older he got, the more he admired and loved him for it. Dale Jr. picked up another six wins in 1998. He won the minor league series championship. In 1999, he finished among the top five in eighteen of thirty-two races and cruised to another title in the top minor league.

Because of Ralph and Dale Sr., the Earnhardts had three generations of NASCAR division champions. In 2000, Dale Jr. moved up to the big leagues. He raced with his dad and for DEI. The year before, Dale Sr. had finished seventh in the overall points race. His goal at the beginning of 2000, as always, was to win a championship. Perhaps helped by the presence of Dale Jr., Dale Sr. almost pulled it off, too. He finished second overall in 2000. The Earnhardts made for a nice story all around.

The relationship was jovial and spirited, but pure father and son in some ways. Dale Sr. was bothered by some of the same things that might cause any father and son to disagree.

"You've got to get up in the morning," he said of Dale Jr. "That's the best time of the day. I was up at 4:30 today. I'm up by 5 every day. Junior . . . he's backsliding. He gets up at 8, 8:30, 9. You miss so much when you get up that late, I tell him. But he just won't listen."[6]

Some saw a spring in Dale Sr.'s step. And there was no greater bounce in 1999 than on April 2.

Dale Sr. finished seventh at the race that day in Texas. Dale Jr. finished first. It marked Dale Sr.'s first NASCAR "Cup" win as an owner. He was clearly more proud, however, as a father.

FROM THE HEART

"I love you," Dale Sr. told his son. "I want to make sure you take this time to enjoy this and enjoy what you accomplished today. You can get so swept up with what's going on around you that you really don't enjoy yourself, so I want you to celebrate."[7]

That was the private Dale Sr. To the media, he quipped, "I'll see how big his head gets now."[8]

In 2000, Dale Sr. raced with both of his sons in the same big league event. Kerry, Dale Jr., and Dale Sr. ran at Michigan Speedway together in August.

TRACK FACT
His thirteen top five finishes in 2000 made for Earnhardt's highest total since 1996.

Members of racing's first family: Dale Jr, Dale, and Kerry Earnhardt before a race in 2000.

Not to be left out of making an impact on the Earnhardt 2000 season, Kelley gave birth to a daughter in September.

The elements in a life spent racing were coming back together for Dale Earnhardt. He'd fractured bones, bumpers, families, and dreams during his early years. He matured. He worked to bring all of them nearer. "It's great to share all of this with your son," he told Montville. "It's exciting. He brings back the excitement. It makes me want to keep doing this."⁹

He and Dale Jr. shared another moment in October of 2000, when Junior wrote a column for nascar.com. It was deep and thankful and appreciative and revealing. When Dale Jr. gave him a chance to read the column before it was posted, Senior was touched.

"He got up and walked right over to me, right in my face," Dale Jr. wrote in *Driver #8*. "He gave me a big hug and told me how much he liked it and I thought for a second we were both gonna cry, which doesn't happen at all with the Earnhardt men."[10]

Father and son seemed to be developing an adult relationship. They may not have shared enough of the young years, but they were making up for lost time. And they were doing so in an intense workplace they both loved.

Meanwhile, the *New York Times* ran a story in August of 2000 about Dale Sr.'s resurgence.

"Earnhardt, Racing's Grumpy Old Man, Is Inching Closer in Winston Cup Points Chase," read the headline.[11]

QUOTABLE
"If someone tells you I'm riding my years out, they're not paying attention."

— Dale Earnhardt on growing old gracefully

"If someone tells you I'm riding my years out," Earnhardt said, "they're not paying attention."[12]

The 2000 race season ended with a whimper for Dale Jr., and everyone, like always, looked ahead to Daytona the following February. Sadly, tragedy would strike there. There was no preparing for the news from the 2001 Daytona 500. It would shock the racing world.

On February 18, 2001, the heartbeat of NASCAR came to a stop.

THE LEGACY

In 2001, Dale Earnhardt was only a few seconds from a safely completed Daytona 500. He was on his way to a great finish, probably in the top three. It certainly wouldn't have hurt his chances of racing toward that elusive eighth championship.

The No. 3 car he drove for Childress that day was strong. Late in the race, only two cars were in front of him. As they neared the turn for home, the No. 15 was in first and the No. 8 was in second. It didn't seem as if Earnhardt would catch them. And maybe he didn't want to, either.

Dale Earnhardt's life came to an end with this crash into the wall at the 2001 Daytona 500.

That might seem odd considering his nature, but those two cars were special to him.

The No. 8 was driven by Dale Jr. and owned by DEI. The No. 15 was driven by Michael Waltrip and also owned by DEI. Waltrip's older brother, Darrell, was the one who battled with Dale Sr. back in the 1980s. During the offseason, DEI added a third "Cup" team for 2000 and needed a driver. Dale Sr. gave his old rival's little brother a shot, even though he hadn't won a race in more than 450 starts.

Watching the final few laps from his favorite chair, Earnhardt must have enjoyed the view. Unfortunately, no one will ever know what he was thinking then. Just before Waltrip took the checkered flag with Dale Jr. second, tragedy struck behind them. As they neared the turn for home, contact launched the No. 3 helplessly from the inside of the track and straight up to the top. The collision with the outer wall was almost a direct hit. It didn't look all that bad to viewers at home. Racing experts were more concerned.

Darrell Waltrip was part of the announcing team that day. He was cheering as his brother enjoyed the best day of his career. He rooted for his brother and celebrated as he crossed the start/finish line. When Darrell was asked if it was better than winning the race himself, he choked up and said it was.

But at the same time, Darrell was also expressing concern for his former rival,

QUOTABLE
"My heart is hurting right now. I would rather be any place right this moment than here. It's so painful."

— Michael Waltrip

Earnhardt. He wondered aloud on the television broadcast : "How about Dale? . . . I just hope Dale's OK. I guess he's all right, isn't he?"[1]

TRAGEDY ON THE TRACK

And that's what everyone thought. Because Earnhardt was inside, everyone could hope for the best. Sadly, it could not have been worse. NASCAR president Mike Helton delivered the awful news, "This is understandably the hardest announcement I've ever had to make. We've lost Dale Earnhardt."[2]

Immediately after his death, shock reigned. The mountain in some people's lives had disappeared. A procession of comments and columns by drivers and pundits and fans followed. Talk of safety and loss and perspective and grief flooded the NASCAR scene. Almost everyone in the country would hear the news.

President George W. Bush called Teresa to offer condolences. The House of Representatives honored Earnhardt's achievements on February 27, 2001. Earnhardt stories landed on the cover of major magazines. NASCAR had lost a legend. No one really knew how to handle that, especially his family.

TRACK FACT
Earnhardt's final race win came on Oct. 15, 2000.

Dale Jr. did what Earnhardts do. Just a week after his father died at Daytona, Dale Jr. got back on the track. He finished forty-third in that week's race, but he raced. "I'm sure he'd want us to keep going, and that's what we're going to do," Dale Jr. said.[3]

Just two years earlier, it was easy to dismiss Junior as a young man who slept too late. In 2001, he found himself in a position similar to his father's in 1973. Both lost their fathers around the time they were becoming adults.

"I lost the greatest man I ever knew, my dad," Dale Jr. wrote in his 2001 book.[4]

It didn't take Dale Jr. long to realize what an impact his father had on him. On July 7, 2001, because NASCAR visits some of its tracks twice in a season, the circuit was back in Daytona for the seventeeth race of the season. Junior won. He won twice more that season and proved to be a very good driver. He has also become the most popular driver at the track, where he's earned tens of millions, just as his dad did.

Junior has appeared on magazine covers, on TV shows, commercials, and has written a book. *Driver #8* looks back at a year in the life (2000) of Dale Earnhardt Jr.

He was more "Little E" then, and his priorities evolved while driving the No. 8 car for DEI. In 2007, Junior made one of the most difficult decisions of his career and life. He decided to leave DEI to race for powerhouse Hendrick Motorsports.

While Dale Jr. lost his dad in 2001, Hendrick lost his son in a 2004 plane crash. There seemed to be a personal connection. Hendrick's operation includes more than 500 employees and four race teams. Among his drivers is none other than Jeff Gordon.

On one hand, Junior may not have wanted to leave the company his dad and Teresa built from scratch and made famous. On the other, he wanted to take advantage of some of his own shifting sands.

Plus, Dale Jr.'s grandfather on his mother's side worked for Hendrick Motorsports when he was involved in racing. Besides, if Dale Earnhardt didn't drive for DEI, it wasn't a given that Dale Earnhardt Jr. had to, either.

"I've always daydreamed about driving for Rick since I started to drive race cars," Dale Jr. said. "I guess if I had my choice in a perfect world, he was kind of always in the lead."[5]

One of the driving forces throughout the negotiations was Kelley Earnhardt Elledge.

Kelley plays a significant role in Dale Jr.'s business dealings. Her husband, Jimmy Elledge, is also from a racing family and is a NASCAR crew chief.

Because of their connection to racing and the name "Earnhardt," Dale Jr. and his sister are still quite

In 2007, Dale Jr. decided to leave DEI and drive for owner Rick Hendrick at Hendrick Motorsports.

famous. Junior's operation includes race teams of his own in the minors and a charitable foundation.

Teresa is still heavily involved in keeping watch over the Dale Earnhardt legacy. Her title at DEI is Chief Executive Officer and President. The operation has grown to occupy 240,000 square feet. It is the home to three Nextel Cup race teams.

There is also a new generation of Earnhardts. Kelley has children. So does Kerry. Kerry's son Jeffrey has even started in the family business. As an eighteen-year-old in 2007, Jeffrey finished fifth in points during a thirteen-race Grand National East Division season.[4] He also appeared in an *ESPN The Magazine* feature. His plan then was to keep racing with the help of his dad and DEI.

In addition to a sprawling complex, DEI has live webcams, racing shops (a gear and transmission shop, a body shop, an engine shop, an engineering shop), and a trophy room. Earnhardt's legacy also lives on in the form of The Dale Earnhardt Foundation, his car dealership, tributes in Kannapolis (the "Dale Trail," Dale Earnhardt Blvd., Earnhardt Road, Dale Earnhardt Tribute Center, and Dale Earnhardt Plaza with its nine-foot-high bronze statue of the sturdy racer), and millions of items of memorabilia.

NASCAR's drivers aren't likely to forget Earnhardt's accomplishments, either. On April 21, 2007,

TRADITION LIVES

Among many legacies, Earnhardt's children Kerry, Kelley, and Dale Jr. have invested in a racetrack complex in Alabama.

Gordon tied Earnhardt's career total by earning his seventy-sixth career win. By winning seventy-six races of his own, Earnhardt made the number almost as famous as the No. 3.

As a way of honoring Earnhardt, Gordon took his victory lap while holding a No. 3 flag. Gordon may have been part of the new school, but he was no longer "Wonder Boy." In June of 2007, he became a father. He came to the game as the anti-Earnhardt, but at least he raced with Earnhardt. That can't be said for the newest generation of NASCAR drivers.

DID YOU KNOW?

Fans can see Earnhardt's childhood hometown of Kannapolis by way of the Dale Trail.

Gordon earned Earnhardt's respect. His gesture merely reminded everyone that the legacy should not be forgotten. Earnhardt was, after all, one of a kind.

On the track, he seemed to see things just a little earlier than everyone else. In a game of split-second decisions that can be short-circuited by fear or desire or anger or goodwill, Earnhardt had a clarity, a feel, that appeared more keen. Earnhardt didn't always need the best car. He just wanted a chance. After all the hard times and harder luck, he could take it from there.

On February 18, 2001, the era came to a close at Daytona International Speedway. It happened just three years after Daytona had been the site of perhaps the biggest feel-good story of the same era.

His is the story of a man with one of the longest sports career arcs ever known. The son of a hard-working driver, he started poor and raced through poverty, divorce and his father's death.

Talent and will were as important as the No. 3 car. Earnhardt drove to achieve more than anyone could have imagined. There was no way to know what was on the other side of those calculated risks, but it made him a household name.

Throughout his career, Earnhardt remained more relevant more often than anyone. His style appealed to so many people, whether they did or didn't like him on the track. There was something about Earnhardt that made people care just a bit more.

He talked tough and drove tougher. Then he found a smoother line. His life gained depth. As he neared fifty, he was clearly enjoying more of his life. There were fewer fears to conquer or dragons to slay.

NASCAR is changing even more quickly. The young guns are younger and the rich are richer.

Who knows if Earnhardt would have enjoyed it if his career, and life, had not ended so abruptly.

Sadly, his life came to an end on the track during a time when it seemed he was enjoying that he had slowed down away from it.

Earnhardt came up like an old-school throw-back who couldn't help but charge forward as fast as he could. It was the ideal fuel mixture for a race car driver.

CAREER STATISTICS

Year	Rank	Starts	Wins	Poles
1975	130	1	0	0
1976	104	2	0	0
1977	118	1	0	0
1978	44	5	0	0
1979	7	27	1	4
1980	1	31	5	0
1981	7	31	0	0
1982	12	30	1	1
1983	8	30	2	0
1984	4	30	2	0
1985	8	28	4	1
1986	1	29	5	1
1987	1	29	11	1
1988	3	29	3	0

Top 5	Top 10	Earnings	Points
0	0	$1,925	0
0	0	$3,085	70
1	0	$1,375	49
1	2	$20,145	548
11	17	$237,575	3,749
19	24	$451,360	4,661
9	17	$324,290	3,978
7	12	$357,270	3,402
9	14	$396,991	3,732
12	22	$509,805	4,265
10	16	$457,658	3,561
16	23	$868,100	4,468
21	24	$1,041,120	4,696
13	19	$739,175	4,256

CAREER STATISTICS

Year	Rank	Starts	Wins	Poles
1989	2	29	5	0
1990	1	29	9	4
1991	1	29	4	0
1992	12	29	1	1
1993	1	30	6	2
1994	1	31	4	2
1995	2	31	5	3
1996	4	31	2	2
1997	5	32	0	0
1998	8	33	1	0
1999	7	34	3	0
2000	2	34	2	0
2001	57	1	0	0

Top 5	Top 10	Earnings	Points
14	19	$885,050	4,164
18	23	$1,307,830	4,430
14	21	$1,029,060	4,287
6	15	$838,385	3,574
17	21	$1,326,240	4,526
20	25	$1,465,890	4,694
19	23	$2,295,300	4,580
13	17	$2,285,926	4,327
7	16	$1,663,019	4,216
5	13	$2,611,100	3,928
7	21	$2,712,089	4,492
13	24	$3,701,390	4,865
0	0	$296,833	132

CAREER ACHIEVEMENTS

- Won seven "Cup" championship titles (1980, 1986, 1987, 1990, 1991, 1993, 1994), tied for most in NASCAR history.

- Became first driver to win a championship the year after being named Rookie of the Year.

- Won 76 career races.

- Led more than 25,000 laps in his career.

- Finished in the top ten in 427 of 677 race starts.

- Earned more than $41 million in career winnings.

- Won four consecutive races in 1987. Won 11 of the first 22 races that season.

- Named the Driver of the Decade (1990s) by ESPN's ESPY Awards.

- Drove for 22 seasons in NASCAR's top circuit.

- Began Dale Earnhardt Inc. in 1980 with his wife, Teresa. "DEI" now owns race teams and Teresa remains CEO and President.

- Took record ten checkered flags at Talladega.

CHAPTER NOTES

CHAPTER 1. MAGIC RIDE

1. Tarik El-Bashir, "Earnhardt Giving It Another Shot," *New York Times*, February 13, 1998. <http://query.nytimes.com/gst/fullpage.html?res=9C04EED F103CF930A25751C0A96E958260&scp=1&sq=Earnhardt+Giving+It+Another+Shot&st=nyt> (August 25, 2008).

2. "1998 Daytona 500," CBS Sports, February 15, 1998.

3. Tarik El-Bashir, "Never on Sunday, Until Now for Earnhardt," *New York Times*, February 16, 1998. <http://query.nytimes.com/gst/fullpage.html?res=9902E1DE163FF935A25751C0A96E958260&scp=1&sq=Never+on+Sunday%2C+Until+Now+for+Earnhardt&st=nyt> (August 25, 2008).

4. Ed Squier interview with Dale Earnhardt, "1998 Daytona 500," CBS Sports, February 15, 1998.

5. Ed Hinton, "The Hunt's Over," *Sports Illustrated*, February 19, 1998, p. 64.

CHAPTER 2. BORN TO RACE

1. Ken Willis, "Dale Was Destined for Greatness," *news-journalonline.com*, February 17, 2002, <http://www.newsjournalonline.com/speed/special/dale/MEMMAIN.htm> (August 25, 2008).

2. Sam Moses, "Dale Turns 'Em Pale," *Sports Illustrated*, September 7, 1987, <http://sportsillustrated.cnn.com/motorsports/news/2001/02/18/earnhardt_1987_flashback/> (August 25, 2008).

3. Leigh Montville, *At the Altar of Speed: The Fast Life and Tragic Death of Dale Earnhardt* (New York: Doubleday, 2001), p. 25.

4. Ibid., p. 26.

5. Bob Knots, "One Driven Family," August 26–28, 1998, *usaweekend.com*, <http://www.usaweekend.com/98_issues/980830/980830earnhardt.html> (August 25, 2008).

6. Leigh Montville, "Dale Bonding," *Sports Illustrated*, December 22, 1999, <http://sportsillustrated.cnn.com/motorsports/news/2001/02/18/earnhardt_and_son_flashback/> (August 25, 2008).

7. Al Levine, "Intense, Intimidating, Irreplaceable," *Atlanta Journal-Constitution*, February 21, 2001.

8. Larry Cothren and the Editors of Circle Track and Stock Car Racing, *Earnhardt: A Racing Family Legacy* (St. Paul, Minn.: MBI Publishing Company, 2003), p. 171.

9. "The Earnhardts," *nascar.com*, December 20, 2002, <http://www.nascar.com/2002/kyn/families/02/01/earnhardts/> (August 25, 2008).

10. Cothren, p. 182.

CHAPTER 3. MERELY A DREAM

1. Josh Pate, "Best Quotes: Dale Earnhardt," *nascar.com*, <http://www.nascar.com/special/earnhardt/stories/quotes.html> (August 25, 2008).

2. Ed Hinton, "Attitude For Sale," *Sports Illustrated*, February 6, 1995, p. 68.

3. Steve Waid, "A True Legend," *scenedaily.com*, March 5, 2001, <http://www.scenedaily.com/news/articles/sprintcupseries/a_true_legend.html> (August 25, 2008).

4. Leigh Montville, *At the Altar of Speed: The Fast Life and Tragic Death of Dale Earnhardt* (New York: Doubleday, 2001), p. 45-46.

5. Bob Knots, "One Driven Family," August 26-28, 1998, *usaweekend.com*, <http://www.usaweekend.com/98_issues/980830/980830earnhardt.html> (August 25, 2008).

6. Sam Moses, "Dale Turns 'Em Pale," *Sports Illustrated*, September 7, 1987, <http://sportsillustrated.cnn.com/motorsports/news/2001/02/18/earnhardt_1987_flashback/> (August 25, 2008).

7. Rick Minter, "Early Years," *Atlanta Journal-Constitution*, February 21, 2001, p. G1.

CHAPTER 4. TRACKING SUCCESS

1. Larry Cothren and the Editors of Circle Track and Stock Car Racing, *Earnhardt: A Racing Family Legacy* (St. Paul, Minn.: MBI Publishing Company, 2003), p. 106.

2. Steve Waid, "A True Legend," *scenedaily.com*, March 5, 2001, <http://www.scenedaily.com/news/articles/sprintcupseries/a_true_legend.html> (August 25, 2008).

3. Ken Willis, "Dale Was Destined for Greatness," *news-journalonline.com*, February 17, 2002, <http://www.news-journalonline.com/speed/special/dale/MEMMAIN.htm> (August 25, 2008).

4. Leigh Montville, *At the Altar of Speed: The Fast Life and Tragic Death of Dale Earnhardt* (New York: Doubleday, 2001), p. 53.

5. Cothren, p. 107.

6. Ed Hinton, "Attitude For Sale," *Sports Illustrated*, February 6, 1995, p. 68.

7. Ibid.

8. Cothren, p. 107.

9. Reporters of the *Charlotte Observer*, *Dale Earnhardt: Rear View Mirror* (Champaign, Ill.: Sports Publishing, 2001), p. 6.

10. Ibid., p. 7.

CHAPTER 5. TEAMING UP

1. Reporters of the *Charlotte Observer*, *Dale Earnhardt: Rear View Mirror* (Champaign, Ill.: Sports Publishing, 2001), p. 6.

2. Steve Waid, "A True Legend," *scenedaily.com*, March 5, 2001, <http://www.scenedaily.com/news/articles/sprintcupseries/a_true_legend.html> (August 25, 2008).

3. Street & Smith's Specialty Publications, *The Earnhardt Collection* (Chicago, Ill.: Triumph Books, 2002), p. 10

4. Ed Hinton, "Attitude For Sale," *Sports Illustrated*, February 6, 1995, p. 68.

5. Leigh Montville, *At the Altar of Speed: The Fast Life and Tragic Death of Dale Earnhardt* (New York: Doubleday, 2001), p. 69.

6. Waid, March 5, 2001.

7. Dale Earnhardt Jr. with Jade Gurss, *Driver #8* (New York, N.Y.: Warner Books, 2002), p. 40.

8. "Dale Earnhardt: Career Totals," *nascar.com*, <http://www.nascar.com/drivers/dps/dearnhar00/cup/index.html> (August 25, 2008).

9. Al Levine, "Intense, Intimidating, Irreplaceable," *Atlanta Journal-Constitution*, February 21, 2001, p. G1.

10. Carrie Seidman, "Youthful Earnhardt Racing Ahead of the Good Old Boys," *New York Times*, August 4, 1980, p. C1.

11. Ibid.

CHAPTER 6. THREE'S COMPANY

1. Larry Cothren and the Editors of Circle Track and Stock Car Racing, *Earnhardt: A Racing Family Legacy* (St. Paul, Minn.: MBI Publishing Company, 2003), p. 107.

2. Steve Waid, "A True Legend," *scenedaily.com*, March 5, 2001, <http://www.scenedaily.com/news/articles/sprintcupseries/a_true_legend.html> (August 25, 2008).

3. Al Levine, "Intense, Intimidating, Irreplaceable," *Atlanta Journal-Constitution*, February 21, 2001, p. G1.

4. Waid, March 5, 2001.

5. Sam Moses, "Dale Turns 'Em Pale," *Sports Illustrated*, September 7, 1987, <http://sportsillustrated.cnn.com/motorsports/news/2001/02/18/earnhardt_1987_flashback/> (August 25, 2008).

6. Street & Smith's Specialty Publications, *The Earnhardt Collection* (Chicago, Ill.: Triumph Books, 2002), p. 32.

7. Ibid., p.33.

8. Reporters of the *Charlotte Observer*, *Dale Earnhardt: Rear View Mirror* (Champaign, Ill.: Sports Publishing, 2001), p. 51.

9. Ibid., p. 49.

10. Waid, March 5, 2001.

11. Leigh Montville, *At the Altar of Speed: The Fast Life and Tragic Death of Dale Earnhardt* (New York: Doubleday, 2001), p. 85.

CHAPTER 7. TITLETOWN

1. Street & Smith's Specialty Publications, *The Earnhardt Collection* (Chicago, Ill.: Triumph Books, 2002), p. 53.

2. Ibid, p. 62.

3. Leigh Montville, *At the Altar of Speed: The Fast Life and Tragic Death of Dale Earnhardt* (New York: Doubleday, 2001), p. 90-91.

4. Street & Smith's Specialty Publications, p. 107.

5. Larry Cothren and the Editors of Circle Track and Stock Car Racing, *Earnhardt: A Racing Family Legacy* (St. Paul, Minn.: MBI Publishing Company, 2003), p. 15.

6. Eric Zweig, *Drive Like Hell: NASCAR'S Best Quotes & Quips* (Buffalo, N.Y.: Firefly Books, 2007), p. 100.

7. Cothren, p. 23.

8. Reporters of the *Charlotte Observer*, *Dale Earnhardt: Rear View Mirror* (Champaign, Ill.: Sports Publishing, 2001), p. 125.

9. Montville, p. 96.

10. Street & Smith's Specialty Publications, p. 183.

11. Ibid., p. 184.

12. Ibid., p. 187.

13. Cothren, p. 73.

CHAPTER 8. RIVALRY BLOOMS

1. Street & Smith's Specialty Publications, *The Earnhardt Collection* (Chicago, Ill.: Triumph Books, 2002), p. 210.

2. Joseph Siano, "Brickyard Struggle Caps Sweep For Jarrett," *New York Times*, February 5, 1995, <http://query.nytimes.com/gst/fullpage.html?res=990CE1D 8133EF936A35751C0A963958260&scp=16&sq=&st=nyt> (August 25, 2008).

3. Larry Cothren and the Editors of Circle Track and Stock Car Racing, *Earnhardt: A Racing Family Legacy* (St. Paul, Minn.: MBI Publishing Company, 2003), p. 96.

CHAPTER 9. AFTERGLOW AND TRAGEDY

1. Leigh Montville, *At the Altar of Speed: The Fast Life and Tragic Death of Dale Earnhardt* (New York: Doubleday, 2001), p. 139.

2. "1997 Daytona 500: Youngest Winner Ever," *nascar.com*, February 10, 2003, <http://www.nascar.com/2003/kyn/history/daytona/02/10/ daytona_1997/index.html> (August 25, 2008).

3. Larry Cothren and the Editors of Circle Track and Stock Car Racing, *Earnhardt: A Racing Family Legacy* (St. Paul, Minn.: MBI Publishing Company, 2003), p. 100–101.

4. Dale Earnhardt Jr. with Jade Gurss, *Driver #8* (New York, N.Y.: Warner Books, 2002), p. 40.

5. Leigh Montville, "Dale Bonding," *Sports Illustrated*, December 22, 1999, <http://sportsillustrated.cnn.com/motorsports/news/2001/02/18/earnhardt_and_son_flashback/> (August 25, 2008).

6. Ibid.

7. Earnhardt, Jr., p. 102.

8. Skip Wood, "Earnhardt Jr. Returns to Site of First Win," *usatoday.com*, March 29, 2001, <http://www.usatoday.com/sports/motor/nascar/2001-03-29-earnhardt-jr.htm> (August 25, 2008).

9. Leigh Montville, *At the Altar of Speed: The Fast Life and Tragic Death of Dale Earnhardt* (New York: Doubleday, 2001), p. 158-159.

10. Earnhardt, Jr., p. 311.

11. Dave Caldwell, "Earnhardt, Racing's Grumpy Old Man, Is Inching Closer in Winston Cup Points Chase," *New York Times*, July 3, 2000, <http://query.nytimes.com/gst/fullpage.html?res=9F06EFD91239F930A35754C0A9669C8B63> (August 26, 2008).

12. Ibid.

CHAPTER 10. THE LEGACY

1. Leigh Montville, *At the Altar of Speed: The Fast Life and Tragic Death of Dale Earnhardt* (New York: Doubleday, 2001), n. pag.

2. "Reaction to Dale Earnhardt's Death," *USA Today*, February 19, 2001, <http://www.usatoday.com/sports/motor/earnhardt/reaction.htm> (August 25, 2008).

3. "Earnhardt Jr. will race Sunday," *espn.com*, February 20, 2001, <http://espn.go.com/rpm/wc/2001/0220/1097157.html> (April 5, 2008).

4. Dale Earnhardt, Jr. with Jade Gurss, *Driver #8* (New York, N.Y.: Warner Vision Books, 2002), p. 348.

5. David Newton, "Earnhardt to Join Gordon, Johnson in Hendrick Stable," *espn.com*, June 13, 2007, <http://sports.espn.go.com/rpm/news/story?id=2902693>.

FOR MORE INFORMATION

ON THE WEB

Dale Earnhardt Inc.'s official Web site:
http://www.daleearnhardtinc.com/

Dale Earnhardt's NASCAR.com page:
http://www.nascar.com/2002/kyn/families/02/01/earnhardts/

Dale Earnhardt Jr.'s official site:
http://www.dalejr.com/

NASCAR.com 50 Greatest Drivers:
http://www.nascar.com/2002/kyn/history/drivers/02/02/
dearnhardt/index.html

FURTHER READING

Cothren, Larry, and the Editors of *Circle Track* and *Stock Car Racing. Earnhardt: A Racing Family Legacy*. St. Paul, Minn.: MBI Publishing Company, 2003.

Elley, K. C. *Hottest NASCAR Machines*. Berkeley Heights, N. J.: Enslow Publishers, Inc., 2008.

Montville, Leigh. *At the Altar of Speed: The Fast Life and Tragic Death of Dale Earnhardt*. New York: Doubleday, 2001.

Street & Smith's Specialty Publications. *The Earnhardt Collection*. Chicago: Triumph Books, 2002.

GLOSSARY

caution flag (yellow flag)—Waved when drivers are required to slow down due to an accident or other hazard on the track.

checkered flag—The flag that is waved as the winner of a race crosses the start/finish line.

circuit—An association or league.

crew chief—The manager of a race team who oversees the mechanics of the car and the crew and is responsible for their performance on race day.

intimidator—A person who causes others to be fearful by his or her actions.

lap—One trip around the track.

manufacturer—A maker of a car or another product.

NASCAR—The National Association for Stock Car Auto Racing, the highest level of stock car racing.

pit crew—The mechanics who work as a team to make adjustments to the car, such as changing tires, during a race.

pit road—The area where pit crews service the cars, usually along the front straightaway.

qualifying—A process in which cars are timed in laps on the track by themselves. The fastest cars getting to start in the best positions for a race.

road course—A racetrack that has both left- and right-hand turns, often run through city streets.

Rookie of the Year—The award given to the best first-year driver on the NASCAR circuit.

short track—A racetrack that is less than one mile long.

sophomore—A competitor's second year in a professional sport.

sponsor—A business that pays money to a race team, generally in exchange for advertising, such as having its logo painted on the car.

sportsmanship—Acting with good conduct and fairness in a sports competition.

standings—A listing of competitors in the order of their performance.

stock car—A standard type of automobile that is modified for use in racing.

superspeedway—A racetrack that is at least two miles in length.

Victory Lane—The winner's circle where the winning driver parks to celebrate after the race.

Winston Cup—The former name of the championship of NASCAR's highest division.

INDEX